little Miss Fun

by Roger Hargreaves

PSS!
PRICE STERN SLOAN

Little Miss Fun is as happy
as a lark.

Except when she is organizing a party.

And then . . .

She is even happier than a lark.

Little Miss Fun simply adores parties.

And she likes to invite lots and lots
of people to her parties.

The other Sunday, there were a lot of people making their way to Little Miss Fun's house.

Mr. Funny was making funny faces.
Mr. Lazy was yawning.
Mr. Clumsy was falling over.

And Mr. Tall was walking in very small steps . . .
So he would not arrive too early!

Mr. Forgetful was not with them.
He was at home, reading a book.
He'd forgotten all about Little Miss Fun's party!

"Never mind,"
laughed Little Miss Fun.
"We can start the party without him!"

She put a record on the record player.

The record went round and round,
and the music played.

Little Miss Fun asked
Mr. Clumsy to dance with her.

And he accepted.

Unfortunately, he stood on her right foot.

"Never mind," she laughed.

Then she ran off to ask Mr. Lazy to dance.

Unfortunately, when he put his head on
her shoulder, he fell asleep.

And almost flattened her!

"Never mind!" she laughed.

In less than an hour,
Little Miss Fun had made everbody dance:

. . . the Rumba and the Samba,

. . . the Rock-and-Roll and the Twist,

. . . the Charleston and the Cha-Cha-Cha.

Then she led everybody out into the garden.

And they danced all around the house.

All the flowers in the garden were trampled.

"Never mind!"
said Little Miss Fun.
"Let's go back indoors."

"Let's play Simon Says . . .,"
she cried.

"Simon Says . . . put your feet in the air!"

There was a loud CRASH!

As Mr. Tall's foot smashed through the windowpane and shattered it!

"Never mind,"
laughed Little Miss Fun.

And she jumped onto the table
so she could pretend to be a clown
and make her friends laugh.

But nobody laughed.

No wonder!

Everbody was exhausted.

They had all fallen asleep.

"Never mind! laughed Little Miss Fun.

And she carried on pretending to be a clown.

Who was she doing it for,
now that everybody was asleep?

Well, she was doing it for a little bird
who had flown in throught the broken window.

But there's someone else she is doing it for,
isn't there?

Why, for you of course!

Because you aren't asleep yet . . .

. . . but you will be soon.